SPELLSWEPT

A Prequel to The Harwood Spellbook

STEPHANIE BURGIS

For Tiffany.
Here's to the power of friendship - and underwater
ballrooms, too!

SPELLSWEPT

A PREQUEL TO THE HARWOOD SPELLBOOK

The evening of the Spring Equinox was cool and balmy, just as the weather wizards had —for once!—reliably predicted. The glittering guest list for the Harwoods' annual ball was exactly to Amy Standish's design.

As she prepared to descend into the lake that gently rippled, reflecting the full moon and stars, outside the grandeur of Harwood House, Amy knew she had organized the most important night of her life so far to absolute perfection. The only tiny, insignificant task left to do was to propose marriage to the right man by the end of this evening. Then she would finally win everything she had ever dreamed of, and it would be utterly *perfect*. She knew it.

There was only one problem with the culmination of all her years of planning...and his name was Jonathan Harwood.

❧

EVERYONE KNEW, OF COURSE, THAT JONATHAN HARWOOD was a problem. That was an open secret in political circles, and a joke in the national papers whenever they most wished to embarrass their political leaders.

The only son of Miranda Harwood—one of the most respected members of the Boudiccate that ruled all of Angland—had actually *refused* to study magic?

His father, like every other gentleman who'd ever married or been born to a powerful Harwood lady throughout history, had been a notable magician until his tragic early death. Jonathan's own place at the Great Library of Trinivantium had been guaranteed to him from birth...yet he'd refused it at eighteen and remained steadfast ever since, turning his back upon centuries of tradition.

Without magical training, he would never be able to make a marriage that benefited his family. He would neither wed nor sire any more shining female politicians to continue the great Harwood legacy; he would never himself rise to the top of the magical hierarchy that was the natural and proper pursuit of every well-born gentleman.

It was inexplicable to the world at large. To the Amy Standish of ten months ago, riding towards Harwood House to take up her appointment as Miranda's new personal assistant, it had seemed quite simply unforgivable.

For a man to turn his back upon his own family...!

At the very thought of it, her whole body had stiffened, her strong, dark brown fingers tightening around the small travelling desk on her lap, where she'd been making notes throughout the journey. It was, of course, a delightful writing desk, made of polished walnut, with leaping horses and owls scrolled in gold along its sides. The various guardians who'd been responsible for her education across the past twenty years had never flinched in passing on the generous allowance that she'd been assigned from her inheritance.

They'd each delivered it to her with scrupulous fairness, just as they'd delivered Amy herself, every year or two, to the next distant relation with an unfortunate obligation to care for her. Then they'd passed the whole sum on to her, with even less well-disguised relief, the moment that she finally reached the age of maturity and they could dust their hands of all obligations towards her forever.

Of course, they'd had their own families to look after. One day, though, Amy would finally establish a family of her own, and then she would be fierce in its protection—and unlike some hopelessly over-privileged and thoughtless young men, she would *never* turn away from them! Even the idea of such a betrayal was—

A flash of blue water caught her gaze, distracting her from her ire, as the thick woodland cleared ahead. *Aha:* finally, the famous Aelfen Mere. It was the site of the late Mr. Harwood's legendary wedding gift to his wife, a spell that had lasted for a mind-boggling three decades by now to create the Boudiccate's most unique and acclaimed festive meeting place.

Over the years, Amy had devoured dozens of newspaper reports about the spectacular masked balls, dazzling theatricals, and world-changing international negotiations that regularly took place beneath the seemingly calm waters of that lake. Emissaries from Angland's allies among the various African nations, the Marathan Empire, and even the widely distrusted new Daniscan Republic had all danced and schemed beneath the blue, along with representatives from the local fairies who shared Angland's landscape in a state of uneasy détente.

Soon, if she succeeded in impressing Miranda Harwood, Amy would find her own place in those negotiations. She had been waiting her entire life for the chance—but of course, being Amy, she hadn't merely waited. She'd spent the last three years making detailed lists of plans for *exactly* how she would manage it.

If there was one lesson Amy Standish had learned in twenty years of being unwanted by her guardians, it was that planning and perfection were the *only* sensible strategies to manage life with her head held high.

And then she met the Harwood family, and every one of her plans was thrown into turmoil.

Now Amy hesitated by the lakeshore on the night of the Spring Equinox Ball, ensnared by memories and hopelessly tangled in emotions...until a familiar voice spoke suddenly behind her.

"*There* you are." Miranda Harwood's words broke through Amy's swirling thoughts. "Still worrying over all the tiny details?" Amusement rippled through her mentor's rich, warm voice as Amy gave a guilty start and stepped back from the lapping waves of the Aelfen Mere. "Trust me, young lady," Miranda said. "If there's one thing I've learned over the years, it's this: no matter how perfectly you've planned anything, something will *always* go amiss."

"Oh, *Mother*," said a second voice. "As if you'd ever allow that to happen!"

Amy could actually hear the eye-roll in that younger female voice...and she couldn't help the rueful smile that tugged at her own lips as she turned around to follow it.

Cassandra Harwood was thirteen years old, bursting with energy, a small and fiercely irrepressible force of nature, and the absolute bane of her famous mother's existence. Mischief glinted in her brown eyes now as she nudged her mother's waist with one impudent elbow. "If anything ever dared go amiss in a party you'd organized, you'd simply look every guest in the eyes and inform them that it had *never happened*. You know they'd be far too intimidated to disbelieve you!"

Miranda cast her own eyes to the night sky. "If only

either of my children felt the same way," she said drily. "Perhaps one day, if I'm extraordinarily fortunate..."

"Standing dreaming outside your own party, Mother?" *That* affectionate voice was adult and male, and so was the jacketed arm that slipped around Miranda's shoulders.

Amy's throat tightened as she tipped her head back. The fond smile she'd been wearing suddenly turned fraught in her own head, a matter of urgent strategic importance. Should she—? Shouldn't she—?

It was a *friendly* smile, she told herself firmly. *Nothing more.*

It was only polite to smile at her mentor's son.

It was...

Oh! His eyes caught hers in the glow of the lanterns that marked out the path from the house to the lake, and she sucked in a breath, her heart lurching horribly.

It was *too much.* It was always too much with Jonathan, because he never even tried to disguise his own feelings for the sake of common sense and self-protection. They shone, unguarded, through his open gaze to pierce her heart with a sweet, aching pain that cut through all of the shields she'd so carefully constructed across the years of her life.

Amy had *plans.* She had a whole future laid out before her, full of professional satisfaction and astonishing achievements that would change the entire nation for the better—a future in which no one would ever again look at Amy Standish and see an unwanted burden, a girl with no proper place in her world.

"We certainly can't stand about dreaming any longer, can we?" Miranda stepped briskly out of her son's embrace. "Just think, Amy: by the end of tonight, you'll be an engaged woman. And then...!"

Amy's smile slipped hopelessly away as Jonathan's steady gaze remained fixed on her face.

Cassandra scowled mutinously. "Well, *I* think Lord Llewellyn's a bore, and not nearly as clever with his magic as he thinks he is. If *I*—"

"You," said her mother through gritted teeth, "are not to mention magic even *once*, Cassandra, from the moment we step into that ballroom! I know you haven't any concern for my feelings, but do you really wish to ruin one of the most important nights of Amy's life?"

"Hmmph." Cassandra's scowl deepened.

But it was Jonathan who shook his head. "Never," he said gently. "Don't worry, Amy. We won't stand in your way. Will we, brat?" He reached over to give Cassandra's shoulder a squeeze.

She leaned into it, her scowl lightening as she looked up at her older brother. The easy warmth and trust that flowed between them tugged at Amy like a hearthfire, pulling her toward that comfort as if...

No! She tipped back on her slippered feet with a jerk. She would *not* give up every dream she'd ever had only to chase a mirage of fleeting happiness. She was a practical woman, not a fool—and he wasn't even asking her to choose him over her political future, was he?

We won't stand in your way, indeed.

Fury swept through Amy's body in a sudden and inexplicable wave that shocked her with its intensity. What was happening to her? Unlike some people, she was always sensible. *He* was the one who made no sense!

He'd spent the last ten months making her smile over her breakfast every morning and playing ridiculous, invented card games with her and Cassandra every night—games that sent all three of them into helpless, full-body fits of laughter like nothing Amy had ever experienced before. She had even fallen somehow, over the months, into the dangerously addictive habit of joining him for long, private walks every day, circling happily around and around the Aelfen Mere as they talked over everything in their heads.

...*Well.* Almost everything, at least.

She had never touched him on any of those walks. Amy's gloved fingers flexed restlessly at her sides, now, at the thought of it. They'd stayed safely within view of Harwood House every time, and Amy had carefully kept her hands to herself, forcing herself to resist every moment of temptation. She would never—*could* never —allow herself to dishonor him in that way.

Mage or not, Jonathan Harwood was a man who deserved to be married, not simply trifled with. But every time Amy had met his blue gaze over the last ten months, the heat of their connection had built higher and higher until it nearly scorched her.

His feelings matched her own; she was sure of it. And he certainly knew all of her plans for tonight. But instead of stepping back from her now as she deserved and closing off all of that hopelessly sincere and irresistible warmth, here he was smiling at her with—with *tenderness* and *understanding*, as if he could read her mind and yet *still* he somehow felt—

Argh!

Amy swung around, her vision blurring, and stepped into the cool, lapping water of the Aelfen Mere, letting it swallow her up before she could lose her mind entirely.

THE FIRST PART OF THE SPELL THAT HAD TRANSFIXED visitors for the past three decades was the entrance to the Harwoods' famous ballroom.

There was no staircase dug into the ground in front of Harwood House, no tunnel leading beneath the lake. Instead, every visitor was required to take a leap of faith: to step, though every sense warned against it, into that rippling blue water and be sucked beneath it. It was a moment of utter helplessness that should have signaled drowning to any who couldn't swim, or at the very least ruin to their elegant ballroom finery.

Instead, after a blur of momentary blindness, Amy landed, as always, dry and secure on a tiled dancing floor that stretched in a vast and generous circle around her. A jangling, ecstatic mingling of fiddles, flutes, and drums swirled through the air, rising up towards the high arched ceiling paned with curving glass that showed off the mysteries of the dark water beyond.

Hundreds of fey-lights floated through the room, lighting up the dazzling jewels of the human dancers, the vibrantly colorful wings and sparkling clothing of the visiting Fae emissaries, and the rich paintings that lined the rounded walls, celebrating the Boudiccate's achievements throughout history. From the expulsion of the Roman invaders through the taming of their Norman would-be conquerors and the more recent international treaties the Boudiccate had struck with empires all around the world, every great moment of the past was lovingly depicted.

In the center of the tiled floor, the great Boudicca herself bared her teeth in victory, laid out in ferocious mosaic beside her second husband, whose magical powers had perfectly complemented her martial and political prowess. Together, they had formed the mold for the nation that grew in their wake, creating an unquestionable law that ruled Angland to this day: pragmatic ladies saw to the politics while gentlemen dealt with the more emotional magic...and no woman could ever be accepted into the Boudiccate without a mage-husband by her side.

"Miss Standish." A familiar, drawling voice spoke nearby, and a glass of sparkling elven wine magically appeared in the smooth, white-skinned hand of the man who'd been awaiting her. He offered it to her with a smile of proprietary satisfaction as his cool green gaze traveled from the curling tendrils of black hair that swung around Amy's ears to the swirling skirts of her gold gown, made of the finest fey-silk. "You look utterly delightful, as always."

"Lord Llewellyn." Smiling warmly, Amy accepted the wineglass from his hand. *No more time for nerves.* Years of plans clicked into motion as she took a first, careful sip of the bubbling wine...and a shiver of air behind her signaled that the Harwood family had arrived.

"My friends!" The tiled floor of the ballroom cleared, and the sparkling assembly fell silent as Miranda Harwood's voice rang through the room.

There was no need for magical amplification, although a number of mages were on hand if required; Miranda Harwood's air of authority was entirely natural. It was one of the things Amy most admired about her and hoped to emulate one day, but for now, she stepped back with everyone else as her mentor swept forward to take control of the room.

"I am delighted to welcome all of you to the Boudiccate's annual Spring Equinox Ball—and on behalf of our government, I'd like to thank my own new assistant, Miss Amy Standish, for organizing it so beautifully. Amy, may I have the honor of introducing you to our guests?" Miranda beckoned her forward as polite applause echoed around the room from Anglish,

Fae, and international attendees alike. "I promise you all," she said confidingly, "that her name will become *extremely* familiar to the nation at large over the next few years—and now, Amy, will you please officially open the ball with my son?"

"Of course." Amy didn't hesitate even as her pulse quickened and an irrepressible flush rose beneath her skin. "If you'll excuse me, my lord..." She passed her wine glass back to Lord Llewellyn with an apologetic smile.

"Have no fears, Llewellyn." Lowering her voice, Miranda gave him a knowing smile. "She'll be all yours soon enough."

"I'm depending upon it." Lord Llewellyn saluted Amy with the glass, his smile perfectly contented.

...And Amy turned, as she'd known she finally must, to Jonathan.

She had been wrong, all those months ago, when she'd imagined that he'd turned his back upon his family. That had been her first of many surprises when she'd arrived at Harwood House ten months ago: to find him not only firmly established in residence like any trusted adult son, but also openly affectionate and ready to assist his mother in anything and everything she wished...except for that one utterly unbending point.

He *would not* study magic as tradition demanded. He was the most loyal and loving son and brother that Amy had ever met—but when it came to that point of principle, he would not budge.

Jonathan Harwood refused to lie about what he truly loved.

One warm, strong hand settled around her waist, and an uncontrollable shiver of reaction rippled through Amy's skin. Still smiling, she lifted her chin and kept her eyes aimed away from his as she twined her right fingers through his left hand and set her own left hand lightly on his broad shoulder, tantalizingly close to the sweet, vulnerable spot where his thick brown hair curled to a stop against his neck.

Too close, too close... How was she supposed to control her feelings when she was standing directly within his arms?

His mother smiled with calm approval, the music swirled back into vibrant life, and Amy and Jonathan swept together towards the center of the dance floor in —unbearably—perfect symmetry.

Fey lights danced overhead like sparkling white stars against the darkness of the deep water outside. Tingles leaped and danced, too, from every point on Amy's skin where her fingers twined around Jonathan's and his hand circled her waist. The muscles in his shoulder shifted against her palm, and she had to draw in a shaking breath.

I can't bear this, she thought as she smiled and smiled over his shoulder at the blurring room beyond. *I can't, I can't...*

"Well done," he murmured as more couples followed them onto the dance floor. "I hope you know how impressed Mother is with the way that you've managed every detail of this ball. She doesn't throw around real compliments lightly—and she usually drives her assistants into the ground."

"Oh, I know." Amy couldn't help a rueful smile; pulled out of her embarrassingly lust-spelled trance, she dared a quick, slanting glance into his lake-blue eyes and found them full of affectionate amusement. "I was quite prepared for that."

"Of course you were." His smile deepened as he twirled her around, the better to show off her footwork to the room.

It was one of the things he seemed to do as easily as breathing—showing off the best in the people around him, always. So it shouldn't have made her chest ache with loss, but it did, of course. It always did.

Why couldn't you have studied magic? Amy closed her eyes for one brief, desperate moment as she twirled back into the circle of his arms. "You're a wonderful dancer." The words felt stilted in her mouth.

"Thank you." His own voice sounded oddly hoarse; his breath ruffled warm and quick against her hair. "It's one of my few skills."

"What rubbish!" Her eyes snapped open. Jonathan always looked confident and at peace with himself—it was one of the most appealing things about him, that warm, steady, reliable presence—but the expression she caught on his face just then looked oddly lost. *Vulnerable.*

The sight made something hurt deep inside her,

and it turned her voice tart with exasperation. "You may let the rest of the world think what they like of you, but I have read the book you're writing, remember? And Cassandra showed me your latest article this morning. You could be the finest history teacher in the country if you wanted to."

"And embarrass Mother even more? I think not." This time, he was the one who averted his gaze, his pale skin flushing. "But thank you for the compliment. You've listened to enough of my tedious history lectures over the past months to earn a place in the Boudiccate just for patience, I should think."

Amy rolled her eyes, relaxing into his arms. "Trust me," she said firmly. "If I'd found them tedious, I wouldn't have asked to hear more of them. And I'll earn my place in the Boudiccate through my own hard work, thank you."

"That part," said Jonathan wryly, "I never doubted."

It was, of course, completely the wrong moment to pass Lord Llewellyn, who danced toward them with the dashing Lady Cosgrave glittering in silver lace in his arms. They both smiled and nodded as they neared, and Lord Llewellyn called across jovially, "Watch out, Miss Standish, or he'll talk your ear off about some dusty old scroll no one's ever wanted to hear of. Unless you'd like me to cast a spell of silence for your sake?"

Amy's teeth gritted behind her smile, even as Jonathan gave an easy laugh and nod in return and the youngest member of the Boudiccate tapped her dance partner's shoulder in mock-reproof.

"Shush now, my lord!" Lady Cosgrave shook her head at Lord Llewellyn indulgently. "You know how much our dear Miranda values his help about the place. And you needn't envy poor Mr. Harwood, you know—you'll have his lovely partner's attention to yourself soon enough, won't you?"

"That is my plan." Smiling, Llewellyn followed her direction to dance gracefully toward the opposite side of the room—where, Amy knew, Lady Cosgrave would be aiming for the Fae ambassadress.

Amy should have been thinking, too, about those delicate trading negotiations that the Boudiccate was trying to strike with the Fae; but it was hard, for once, to care about such details as her lips pressed tightly together, trying to hold back an entirely impolitic response to her own intended fiancé.

"Is something amiss?" Jonathan frowned, pulling her a fraction closer as he inspected her face. "You look..."

"It's nothing." If Jonathan was willing to laugh off Llewellyn's comment, so should she; it made no sense to feel this sort of rage over an insult so casual and unthinking, especially when it came from a man whom she should forgive whenever possible, for expediency's sake.

And yet...

"Are you certain?" Still frowning, he cast a quick glance up at the dark panes of glass above them and the deep waters outside. "I would offer to accompany you outside for some air, but in this particular case..."

"I'd rather not drown tonight, thank you." Her lips tugged up in a reluctant half-smile. "I wouldn't mind a sip of wine, though."

And a reason to make myself let go of you, she added silently. She had no choice; she *had* to sort her rebellious thoughts back into order before she could make any terrible misstep—and it would be infinitely easier without the perilous distraction of his warmth surrounding her.

So it was entirely illogical to feel a pang of loss when he immediately released her. "Of course." He stepped back, waving her toward the refreshments table at the far side of the room. "Shall we?"

Her waist felt cold where his hand no longer touched her. She took his arm instead in the lightest of holds and walked sedately by his side through the swirling dancers, smiling and nodding to every couple they passed. She could name and describe every one of the guests after all the hours she'd spent on careful research before writing out the invitations. If put to the test, she could have recited a whole litany of facts and personal details about each of them, including their views on at least half a dozen of the most pressing political issues facing the Boudiccate this spring.

So it was easy to make small talk to the dancers who paused to converse; easy to subtly nudge those conversations in exactly the right directions for Miranda's aims; easy, too, to smile and warmly enthuse at those guests while never aiming a single look at the man whose arm she held, even as awareness rippled through her with every move he made.

When they reached the long refreshments table, it grew easier yet, because the first thing she saw there made her relax into outright laughter: Cassandra Harwood with her back to the dancers and a look of guilty glee on her face, attempting to fit an entire cake into her mouth.

"You'll be sick!" Amy said, wincing as she hurried forward. "Or worse, spill crumbs on your gown."

"Worth it," Cassandra mumbled around the cake. "I only just managed to sneak away." She wiped her arm across her mouth as she gulped the cake down, scattering crumbs across her pale blue gown without any visible shame. Recalcitrant strands of thick brown hair were already beginning to tumble free from her chignon, as irrepressible as Cassandra herself. "I thought I'd never make it over here, Mother had such a grip on me."

"Introducing you 'round again?" Jonathan smiled ruefully at his little sister. "You'd think she must have introduced you to every possible political mentor in the nation by now, wouldn't you?"

"She was probably hoping they'd forgotten me since the last time." Cassandra smirked back at him.

Amy rolled her eyes in exasperation. "Do you have *any idea* what I would have given to have Miranda Harwood introduce me to political mentors when I was your age?"

"Nearly as much as I'd give to make her stop?" Cassandra's face tightened as she reached for another cake, her gaze sliding away from Amy's.

Jonathan shifted closer to his sister. "Here, brat." He pointed past her at a different plate, his voice gentling. "That one has a liquid chocolate filling. If it accidentally spills all over your gown, well then...you'll simply have to have some time away to change, won't you?"

Cassandra let out a choked laugh—and Amy realized, with a start, that the girl was fighting to hold back an actual sob, for the first time since they'd met. Cassandra's usual unquenchable self-confidence might make life at Harwood House a challenge at times, when she opposed Miranda's firm expectations for what seemed the mere joy of showing off her independence—but to see that fierce, spiky girl on the brink of tears now felt more than worrying. It felt *wrong.*

It was automatic for Amy to angle herself at Jonathan's side, blocking his little sister from the view of the crowd for the sake of the family and the evening's entertainment. But it was a deeper and less rational urge—one that Amy couldn't resist—to reach out once they were safely shielded from view and cup one hand lightly against Cassandra's cheek, stroking away that first tell-tale tear as a wave of fierce protectiveness welled up within her.

"Tell me," Amy said with soft intensity. "Did someone say something to hurt you? Or..."

Cassandra shrugged irritably, lowering her eyes,

but she didn't shift away from Amy's tentative touch. Instead, she leaned into it. "It's just...it never changes! No matter how many times I tell Mother what I want, she *will not listen*. She simply carries on the way she always does, sweeping everyone around her into doing whatever *she's* decided is best. *You* know," she said, appealing to Jonathan. "It's one thing when she's doing it for the whole nation, but—"

"Shh." He gave her a warning look and stepped closer, blocking her in, as a chattering group of guests stepped up behind them to pick through the assorted cakes and sweetmeats.

"Perhaps...?" Amy gestured toward the rounded wall that curved behind the refreshments table. A transparent pane of glass inserted between the paintings there created a perfect lookout point and excuse.

Together, she and the two younger Harwoods drifted toward it, Cassandra safely flanked on both sides by Amy and Jonathan. Smiling brightly as they all reached the glass, Amy made a show of pointing at the dark water outside...and dropped her voice as she studied the girl beside her: the second life-tilting surprise to have greeted her when she'd first arrived at Harwood House ten months earlier.

By every right, Cassandra Harwood should have loathed Amy on first sight. Not only had Amy been an interloper upon Cassandra's family home, but Miranda Harwood had made her own delighted approval of her new assistant abundantly clear from Amy's first month onward.

It was a gift she'd never dared to expect from the woman she'd idolized all her life—but that didn't stop Amy from wincing with discomfort whenever she heard Miranda slip into outright comparisons during the epic battles that raged between mother and daughter.

"For goodness' sake, why can't you simply model yourself on Amy?"

She wouldn't have blamed Cassandra for turning against her completely. Instead, the younger girl had welcomed Amy from the first, drawing her unquestioningly into the family's private entertainments, teasing her with exuberant warmth, inviting herself into Amy's room for tea and confidences, and treating Amy in every way like her own triumphantly-acquired and inherently lovable older sister.

It was entirely unexpected; it was unbearably sweet; and much as she'd discovered with Cassandra's older brother, Amy found that she had no natural defense against such open and genuine affection. Unlike anyone else she'd ever met, neither of the Harwood siblings ever expected her to prove herself to them in any way. In return, she found she couldn't bear to witness either of them suffer, no matter what the cause.

She bit back a sigh now as her loyalties pulled hard against each other, straining her resolution to breaking-point.

Of course she'd always known that Cassandra chafed at her mother's ambitions for her—their battles were legendary, loud and inescapable, pitting their twin wills against each other—but it was the one subject that Amy and Cassandra had never discussed in all their afternoons and evenings of cake and gossip. Amy would never betray her mentor, and Cassandra knew it.

Now, though, Amy gave in at long last to inevitability. "Cassandra," she said quietly, leaning closer, "I'll speak to your mother for you if you'd like. You know she can't truly force you to become a politician. If you dig in your heels and simply refuse to take that path, then nothing she does can compel the Boudiccate to accept you. If you only wait until you're a grown adult and can choose another vocation for yourself—"

"I've *chosen*," Cassandra said with bitter emphasis. "That's the problem. Hadn't you worked it out yet?"

"I beg your pardon?" Amy blinked, looking to Jonathan for answers.

His brows knitted together; he shook his head slightly in return. Clearly, it was Cassandra's truth to share.

"Haven't you heard me going on and on about magic?" The younger girl's smile was wobbly. "Obsessions run in our family, you know. Mother's politics, Jonathan's history, and my..."

"Magic?" Amy repeated, baffled. Of course she had heard Cassandra give loud opinions on the matter—she was surprisingly well-informed on that masculine topic, considering that her only brother had turned so famously against it—but Amy had always assumed that Cassandra's own professed interest was just another way to needle her overbearing mother. It was certainly an effective strategy, since Miranda lost her temper every time Cassandra brought up the subject in conversation.

"You...want to study the history of magic, you mean? As your profession?" Amy took a deep breath, absorbing the startling news. "Well, I know that isn't what Miranda's planned for you"—and it would certainly raise eyebrows in society for a lady to take so much interest in that subject, even if it was all safely couched in history—"but perhaps, if we angle it just the right way—"

"No!" The word burst out of Cassandra like an explosion, loud enough to draw attention from the groups nearby.

"Careful," Jonathan warned in a soft whisper. "If someone hears you—"

"I don't care!" She wrapped her arms around her chest, misery seeping out of every pore. "Oh, I know it's supposed to be a shameful secret, but if I have to hold it in much longer—"

"Look out of the window, quickly." Gently, Amy nudged Cassandra's shoulder, turning her to hide her face from the assembly. "Now explain it all to me. Carefully, please, since I'm so slow tonight."

"I..." Cassandra hiccupped on a sob. Her lips twisted, and with a sudden, jerky move she thrust her right hand forward, palm upwards. "Just *look*!"

She whispered something under her breath too

quietly for Amy to catch the words...and a bright spark of fire suddenly appeared in her palm, hidden from the rest of the ballroom between her body and the glass.

Shock stopped Amy's breath. She almost staggered. *Cassandra was casting magic.*

Amy's gaze flew instinctively to Jonathan's face, expecting her own stunned disbelief to be reflected there. This couldn't really be happening, could it?

But astonishingly, he wasn't even looking at the incredible—unheard of! unimaginable!—event taking place only inches away from them. Instead, his blue eyes were fixed steadily on her face, faint lines of worry creasing his expression.

He was waiting, she realized, to see how she would react—and whether she was, after all, a safe person to trust with such an explosive secret.

Good God. She swallowed convulsively, her breath returning in a rush. If anyone else found out...

How long had the Harwood family been keeping this secret? If the news ever reached the rest of the Boudiccate—much less the newspapers!—that Miranda Harwood's own daughter was flouting every law of nature by daring to cast magic of her own...

"Miss Standish!" Lord Llewellyn's voice rang out behind her, and Amy spun around with a gasp of horror.

To her deep relief, she felt Jonathan step quickly behind her, providing an extra shield between Llewellyn and his sister.

Amy pinned a bright, dazzling smile on her face and snapped out her fan with one hand, creating even more of a visual barrier, while she extended her other hand in greeting. "Is it time for our first dance, my lord?"

"At last." Smiling with proprietary satisfaction, he took her proffered hand—then cast a brief, dismissive nod in Jonathan's direction. "Harwood." His eyes widened as Cassandra stepped out from behind her older brother, her chin held high and her hands —*thank goodness*—safely empty. "And Miss Harwood! An honor to see you, always."

This time, his nod was closer to a bow. *Of course*. An entirely inappropriate, semi-hysterical giggle fought its way up Amy's throat as she watched the rapid calculations unfurling in Llewellyn's clever gaze.

Jonathan, in his eyes, was unimportant—no rival in magery or romance and thus entirely beneath consideration. Cassandra, on the other hand, was publicly understood to be her mother's intended successor within the Boudiccate and one of the future rulers of the nation, so he didn't dare offend her.

If he'd had even the slightest idea...

"Miss Standish?" Llewellyn raised his eyebrows at her. "Are you quite well?"

"Of course, my lord." Amy gave her fan a brisk wave to cool her face, then let it fall back on the knotted golden cord that she wore about her wrist, matching the golden silk of her skirts. "I'm only looking forward to our dance."

"As am I." Bowing to Cassandra—and ignoring Jonathan completely—Llewellyn drew her forward to join the other couples on the tiled floor.

Over his shoulder, Amy watched Jonathan loop a protective arm around his sister, whispering something that made her nod and close her eyes, resting her head against his jacketed chest. When he glanced back up, his gaze caught Amy's through the crowd.

Her feet stumbled in their moves.

Curse it. She lowered her eyes quickly, wrenching herself back into the moment and to her dance partner.

Lord Llewellyn was her *future* partner in every way, and she could never let herself forget that salient fact. Breathing deeply, she forced herself to take careful note of his hand at her waist—pleasantly firm, not over-tight—and the long fingers that he'd tangled possessively with hers. It all felt perfectly agreeable. He danced with skill.

He did everything with skill, in fact. According to Miranda, he was widely considered to be one of the most promising mages of his generation, predicted to rise high among their ranks. All that he truly required now was a wife like Amy with a prominent family name and the political acumen to become a star in her own right. Together, they had the potential to rise into England's ruling echelon.

"And he's even rather handsome," Miranda had finished, when she'd given Amy her private summation the day before introducing the pair. *"Which one*

can't always count upon, you know. Not everyone is so fortunate."

Her smile had turned unwontedly wistful at that statement—and Amy had glanced beyond her at the portrait of the late Mr. Harwood that hung in Miranda's study, an unusually sentimental ornament for that practical place of business.

Miranda *had* been fortunate in her own husband's appearance, judging by both that portrait and the two children who had been born to their match—but she, too, had married for strategy, not for love. It was the only sensible way to choose a partner for any woman with intelligence and ambition—and of course, if one chose wisely, respect and mutual assistance would eventually turn into real affection. It was everything that Amy had ever hoped for in a match.

So she forced the Harwoods and their revelations from her mind to smile up at Lord Llewellyn now and give him the disciplined focus that he would deserve throughout their lives together. "Are you enjoying the evening, my lord?"

"Very much." He gave an assessing glance around the room and nodded approvingly. "You really haven't missed anyone, have you? If you wouldn't mind aiming this way for a bit..." He maneuvered her adroitly to one side, moving smoothly across the room.

Amy slid a discreet glance of her own in that direction, keeping the warm, open smile on her face. "Are we intercepting Mr. Westgate?" she murmured.

His own smile unflinching, Llewellyn twirled her

adeptly around the next couple in their path. "I want to make certain he'll be watching the demonstrations later on."

"Aha." Amy slipped back into place in his arms, her mind humming back into motion as she returned to her usual, non-Harwood-distracted work.

Llewellyn was speaking, of course, about the *magical* demonstrations, when the younger mages would take turns displaying their talents for the delight of the assembly. A traditional moment at the end of any ball, it was the perfect opportunity for young, ambitious gentlemen to show off their strengths—both to the older men who might advance their magical careers and to the eligible young women who might be persuaded to consider them as marital partners. At a ball like this, it also served a vital function for the nation: to impress diplomats from other realms with the ongoing power of England's magecraft, which had turned back so many attempted invasions in the past.

Westgate was one of the Boudiccate's own officers of magic, and among the highest-ranking of that elite force. Amy might not know a great deal about magic herself, but she knew all about power and influence, so she was fully prepared by the time they met a moment later.

"Mr. Westgate!" Beaming, she tugged Lord Llewellyn to a halt before a tall, lean man with dark brown skin and graying, close-cut hair, who stood by the sidelines sipping a glass of elven wine without any noticeable enjoyment. "I am delighted to see you here, sir. Is everything to your satisfaction?"

Westgate's eyebrows rose as he lowered his wine. "Miss...Standish, was it not?"

Amy nodded, intensifying the warmth of her smile. "Mrs. Harwood was so pleased when you accepted her invitation. She thinks very highly of your work, you know."

"Indeed." His eyebrows, if anything, notched a little higher. "Perhaps she ought to listen to a bit more of my advice, then."

Luckily, Amy had been quite prepared for that crotchety response, because whenever Miranda spoke of Lionel Westgate, her words of reluctant praise had invariably been followed by the conclusion: "...*even if he is the crankiest mage in all Angland.*"

So unlike Llewellyn, she didn't twitch at Westgate's words. Instead, she tipped her head to one side with a look of warm conspiracy. "Now, Mr. Westgate. You know you can't expect the members of the Boudiccate to respond to instruction as if they were students at the Great Library. They have to discuss important matters and make decisions amongst themselves—but they always take your advice into account."

"Ha." He gestured with his nearly-full wine glass at the arched ceiling high above them, beyond all of the dazzling fey-lights. "Then why are we still holding events here, do you think? When I've warned her time and time again..."

At that, Amy blinked. "I beg your pardon?"

He shook his head. "No one denies old Harwood's genius. But the spell must need reinforcement eventually—it's a miracle it's lasted this long without him here to keep an eye on it!—and yet she won't let any other mages inspect it for safety. Calls the idea an insult to her husband's memory, if you can believe it!"

The water outside the thin panes of glass suddenly seemed even darker, as if it were squeezing tighter around the ballroom as discomfort tightened Amy's chest.

How many years had it been since Mr. Harwood's death, now? Five? If his spell collapsed now...

She took a deep, sustaining breath, carefully maintaining the easy good humor of her expression. "Aren't we fortunate, then, to have so many brilliant mages here with us tonight for our protection?" As if only just then reminded of him, she gave a small start and turned back to her dance partner. "Oh! You are acquainted with Lord Llewellyn, are you not, Mr. Westgate?"

"Llewellyn." Westgate nodded briefly, his expression unreadable.

"Sir." Llewellyn's smile was broad and confident. "A pleasure to meet you again. Good work with that band of kelpies last month."

"Them?" The older man shrugged irritably. "Those were hardly a challenge for a whole team of us together."

"Well, I've been working on a spell that might help in cases like those, actually." Llewellyn took a step closer. "It might even turn that into a one-man operation."

"Oh really?" Westgate's eyes narrowed as he raised his wineglass, preparing for another sip. "Planning to present it tonight at the demonstrations?"

Llewellyn nodded with exactly the right look of deferential respect. "I'd be grateful for your thoughts on it, if you wouldn't mind."

"Hmm." Westgate took a long sip of elven wine. "Well, don't ask me now, boy. We'll see what I think after I watch it in action."

Llewellyn opened his mouth; Amy squeezed his arm warningly. With a sigh, he relaxed and stepped back, taking her cue. "Thank you, sir. I'll look forward to it."

"Just don't collapse this place around us when you do it!" Westgate called after them as they swept back onto the crowded dance floor.

Lowering her voice as they joined the other dancers, Amy asked, "Is that a real possibility, do you think?"

"Nonsense." Llewellyn's lips twisted with amusement. "You needn't worry about any of Westgate's mutterings, Miss Standish. 'The Raven of Doom', you know—that's what all of the Great Library students call him, because he's always harping on about the worst that might happen."

He shook his head, leading her gracefully across the floor. "It's as you told him yourself: before the Boudiccate decides on anything, they'll always discuss it amongst themselves and take various mages' opinions into account. I'll wager they've had plenty of private inspections of this place in the last few years. They simply didn't want to tell old Westgate they'd chosen someone else for the job, to keep themselves safe from all his cawing about it."

"Mm." Amy kept her tone perfectly neutral, but her eyebrows wanted to knit into a frown. She kept her expression clear with an effort, conscious of every potential watching eye.

Of course Llewellyn knew far more about magic than she did—but Amy knew a good deal about people. Lionel Westgate's hair might be graying with age, but he was full of energy and sharp intelligence. He hadn't struck her as a man prone to unfounded worries.

Still, her future husband was right: the Boudiccate always took important magical questions to their council.

Except when it comes to Miranda's family. The thought shivered through her with a whisper of unease as she suddenly remembered that impossible, dancing flame cupped in Cassandra's hand. Miranda certainly hadn't discussed *that* with her fellow members of the Boudiccate, had she? Amy had lived for ten months with the Harwood family without even guessing at the secret—and if Cassandra hadn't lost her temper, it might never have come out at all.

Miranda might battle fiercely with her equally strong-minded children, but she would never betray either of them to outsiders. That had been proven to the world when she'd neither disowned Jonathan as expected, nor even banished him from the family home when he'd refused his place at the Great Library and struck out on his own, unsanctioned career path.

"*You* hit the right notes with him, though," Llewellyn said, "as usual." He pulled her a fraction closer with unmistakable possessiveness. "Just think how well we'll do together," he murmured into her ear. "With your political skills and my magic...what *can't* we hope for?"

The answer died, unspoken, in Amy's mouth as another couple circled past.

Jonathan Harwood was dancing with Lady Cosgrave this time, with the ease of long acquaintance. Lady Cosgrave—by far the most approachable member of the Boudiccate—was clearly trying to lecture him with the tone of an older sister, while he smiled and parried all of her points and made her laugh despite herself.

Following Amy's gaze, Llewellyn let out an aggravated huff of breath. "Incredible, how he's wormed his way into everyone's good graces."

Amy's eyebrows rose; using the excuse of a sweeping turn, she pulled subtly back within his embrace. "I don't believe Mr. Harwood is trying to gain anything from Lady Cosgrave or any of the other members of the Boudiccate."

"Ha. I went to school with him, you know, before any of us were old enough for the Great Library. The son of one of the oldest magical families in the realm, and he wouldn't even pretend to take an interest in the subject. He should have been a laughing-stock from day one—anyone else would've been!—but somehow, by the end of our first year, he'd actually talked everyone into thinking him 'such a good fellow,' despite everything."

Llewellyn shook his head in open disgust. "Of course we all expected it to come crashing down for him in the end, when he'd finally have to fall into line and head to the Great Library with the rest of us, but no...he *still* wouldn't budge. And he didn't even lose anything for it!"

Amy narrowed her eyes, studying her partner's face warily. "Hasn't he paid a significant price by not attending? He'll never rise in the world as you and the others will."

"Just look at him," Llewellyn said bitterly. "Does he seem to you as if he's suffering for everything he tossed away? When you think of every man who'd fight and strive for the opportunities *he* was born with..."

Aha. Well, there it was: for all that Llewellyn's family was perfectly respectable and respected, they were certainly no Harwoods. Not a single woman in his family, past or present, had ever represented the nation as a member of the Boudiccate; no gentleman among them had ever risen to the highest magical posts in the realm. Llewellyn's own ambition must have nearly choked him when he'd watched Jonathan Harwood reject it all—and Amy couldn't help but understand how he had felt.

But that wasn't what made her breath catch in sudden realization. *Oh!*

Finally, it all made sense.

"What could make any man so careless?" Llewellyn muttered.

Amy didn't answer him aloud. But in her head she silently corrected him: *Not 'what.'* Her gaze scanned through the crowd until it fastened on a head of thick, curling brown hair—the same hair that ran all through the Harwood family—because the right question to ask, of course, was actually: *'Who?'*

Jonathan Harwood was the least careless person she knew, but what he cared about, unlike Llewellyn, wasn't power. It was family. And that was why she'd never truly understood his decisions—until now.

He could always have studied his beloved history on the side while dutifully carrying on the family legacy in public...but only if he weren't convinced that someone else deserved to take on the weight and power of that legacy herself. How soon had he realized his younger sister's passion?

It was impossible, unthinkable for any woman to study magic...

But...not quite so impossible, perhaps, after Jonathan Harwood had taken that first public step to prepare his family and his cohort for that change.

Amy could barely breathe as her thoughts whirled around that single, earth-shaking point, re-sorting and reassembling themselves around a concept she'd never dared to imagine before.

"Miss Standish?" The music was coming to a halt; Amy blinked back into the world to find Lord Llewellyn impatiently repeating himself, a look of barely-veiled irritation on his handsome face. "I *said*, shall we make the announcement at the end of this evening? Or—"

Announcement? Her mind still full of swirling schemes, it took Amy a moment to absorb his words. Then they clicked into place. "Of course!" she said, injecting warm enthusiasm into her words. "Our announcement."

Their wedding announcement—that must be what he meant. Of course she hadn't actually proposed to him yet; she'd planned to do so, officially, during one of their three dances across the evening. But it would be foolish to be irritated by his presumption now when everyone knew that she would ask, and everyone knew, likewise, what his answer would be.

"Ye-e-es..." His frown deepened even more as he released her, holding out one arm to escort her off the dance floor. "So your answer to my question is...?"

"The end of the evening," she said quickly. "After the demonstrations. That would be the perfect timing."

Every guest would be assembled and attentive at that point—and, better yet, it would give her plenty of time to compose herself first, after all the revelations of this evening.

Smiling brightly, Amy patted his arm, stepped away from her intended, and slipped into the crowd before he could stop her.

She didn't aim for Jonathan or Cassandra Harwood this time. That way lay only more perilous confusion. Instead, she moved on a carefully selected path from one guest to another, mingling, laughing, asking thoughtful questions, and making certain each time to casually bring up Miranda's most favored projects before moving on. It was a dance of its own, although she'd left the physical dance floor behind her. The careful shifting of moods and opinions, the thrill of persuasion and the buzz of the challenge—it all filled her with a brimming energy that felt more sparkling and effervescent than even the finest elven wine.

This was the purpose that she'd been born for—and when she met Miranda in the midst of her rounds an hour later, the undisguised approval on her mentor's face warmed Amy more than any fire. Smiling, Miranda drew her aside to murmur into her ear.

"Mrs. Seabury," she said, referring to the oldest and most intimidating member of the Boudiccate, "just stalked across the room to ask me where I'd found my new assistant...*and* to offer me more than a few political favors if I'd release you to her service instead!"

Amy's eyes widened, her heart giving a sudden lurch as that lovely warm sense of security slipped suddenly away from her. "What did you tell her?"

"What do you think?" Miranda laughed and gave Amy's shoulder a reassuring pat. "Trust me, my dear.

Old Seabury lost her ability to talk me out of anything that really mattered years ago. I have *far* greater plans for you than simply to move on to another assistantship! Once you're safely betrothed and we can start you on your way..." She tilted her head, her voice dropping even lower. "Is everything arranged to your satisfaction there?"

She meant, *Have you proposed?*

Ah. Amy's fingers tightened around her wineglass. Of course she should have taken care of it by now...but then, Llewellyn had rather bypassed that necessity, hadn't he? Still, she *would* issue her proposal by the end of the evening to make it official. So... "We'll make our announcement after the demonstrations."

"Excellent. Perfectly timed, as usual." Smiling warmly, Miranda nudged Amy around and raised her voice as the Fae ambassadress approached in a glittering blur of wings and color. "Your Eminence! Have you met my new assistant yet? She arranged this entire evening, you know..."

Amy dived back into the political whirl with pure exhilaration and didn't emerge again until thirty minutes later, when a firm hand closed around her arm just as she was shifting away from a large group. It was Llewellyn's hand, and when she turned, she found his smile tinged with irritation. "I've hardly even glimpsed you tonight. Aren't we due another dance by now?"

"I—yes, of course." Swallowing down a sigh—she'd been aiming at a particular target in her next group—

Amy nodded, remembering Miranda's advice. *Time to take care of those final details.* Once her proposal had been safely issued and accepted, everything would be perfectly sorted according to her plans. After all, once their betrothal was official, she *couldn't* back out from the decision—not without ruining her political prospects beyond repair. A politician's word was her bond.

And there was certainly *no* reason to feel any panic about that! So—

"Miss Standish," said Jonathan Harwood, and Amy turned to him in a rush of relief even as Llewellyn's grip tightened uncomfortably around her arm.

"Mr. Harwood." She beamed at him even as she gave her constrained arm a discreet tug. "Does your mother require my assistance?"

"Ah...yes, I'm afraid. It's a family issue." He nodded to Llewellyn, his face carefully neutral but his gaze fixed on the other man's still-tight grip around Amy's bare brown arm. "Apologies, Llewellyn, but it shouldn't take too long."

"Don't you think it could wait, then, until I've had my turn?" Llewellyn's grip didn't loosen as he narrowed his eyes. "I appreciate that your purpose in life nowadays is to run your mother's errands, but—"

"*Actually*," Amy said, with a firm and undisguised yank that took Llewellyn by surprise and threw him off-balance, "Mr. Harwood's purpose in life is the study of the Daniscan invasion, just as *my* purpose tonight is to assist his mother in whatever she may need. You should read some of Mr. Harwood's published articles, Lord Llewellyn. They really are quite enlightening."

She didn't even attempt to hide her flare of irritation as she twitched herself free, a pointed rebuke in her gaze. There was a duty of attention owed to one's partner, certainly, but there was also a duty of respect between equals. She would *always* make her own decisions for herself as well as—in the future, with luck—for the whole of Angland.

Llewellyn might have just exposed a temper, but he had a brain, too—and he was far too clever to misread her message. As she watched with expectantly raised eyebrows, his cheeks thinned and his lips clamped together, visibly restraining an untoward response. Still, he lowered his eyes a moment later without letting any more thoughtless words escape. "As you say." He sighed. "I'll look forward to our dance, Miss Standish...the very moment that you *are* free to enjoy yourself."

Good. Amy took a deep, reassuring breath. For a moment, she'd actually wondered...but no.

"I'll rejoin you as soon as possible," she promised —and, with a firm smile, took Jonathan's arm. "Lead on, Mr. Harwood, do."

Jonathan didn't speak at first, as they moved smoothly together through the crowd; when he did speak, his voice was muted. "There must be a better one that you can find."

"I beg your pardon?" Amy slanted a glance up at his face—and realized, with a start, that for the first time in her memory, Jonathan Harwood was utterly furious. The emotion radiated through every inch of his body and blazed out through his eyes, even as his face remained perfectly expressionless—a skill and restraint he must have practiced a great deal after all those years spent away in boarding school with other boys who felt as Llewellyn did about him. "A better what?" she asked, with genuine curiosity.

He gave a quick, jerky shrug. "A better *option*, I mean, for you! I've been doing my best to hold my tongue about it, but Llewellyn isn't good enough, and you know it."

What? Amy's breath stopped in her chest for one stunned moment. Then it rushed back into place, propelled by sheer rage. "*This* way," she said, and altered their direction. Smiling with all her might, she swept a path through the crowd to the next available pane of glass...where she was finally, *finally* free to drop her furious smile and openly glare at the dark water beyond.

"Are you actually commenting on my *options*?" she demanded in a ferocious whisper. "*You*?"

He gave an unmistakable flinch. Then his jaw squared and he stepped closer to the glass, his jacketed arm brushing lightly against her own and sending aggravating sparks along her skin. "Yes, I am," he said firmly. "I know Mother thinks he's fated to rise high in his career, but I can tell you, I've known him for years, and Cassandra's right—he isn't nearly as good at magic as he thinks he is."

"And you're holding yourself up as a judge on that?" Fury nearly choked her. She squeezed her eyes shut, trying to hold herself back.

Of course he knew how she felt—he *had* to know. No one had ever accused Jonathan Harwood of being anything less than extraordinarily intelligent. That was what had famously driven his parents so wild with frustration. For him to utter such a remark after ten months of unmistakable warmth, bone-deep connection and a longing so desperate that some nights it had nearly choked her...

"I understand and respect why you made your own decisions," she said with tight control, her eyes still shut. "But *do not* taunt me about them now!"

"*Taunt?*" He didn't touch her, but she could feel the breath of frustration that he expelled, ruffling against her upswept hair. "What are you talking about?"

If they'd been alone, she would have tipped her head against the glass in frustration. They were in public, though, and in full view of the crowd, so she kept her figure upright and relaxed. "You know perfectly well what I mean," she said bitterly. "I don't have the freedom to choose the man I most admire. That is not an *option* for me, as you so charmingly put it, because *you* chose a different path for your own reasons. So don't pretend that I need to please *you* with my marital choice now! That," she finished wearily, "is asking far too much of me."

There. Her shoulders slumped. She'd said what she

needed to say. Now she would simply endure his answer, move back into the whirl of the ball, and...

But no answer came after all. Finally, she opened her eyes to investigate.

Reflected in the dark glass before her, his own eyes were wide and stunned-looking. "I...what?" he demanded. "*What*?"

She stared at his reflection, wordless with confusion.

Jonathan raked one hand through his thick brown hair, rumpling it hopelessly out of shape. She wished she didn't find it so appealing. "Miss Standish—*Amy*," he said, his voice hoarse. "Are you telling me...would you have actually desired...?"

She shook her head in pure confusion. "What did I say that was so difficult to understand?"

"But..." He took a deep breath, his broad chest rising and falling.

"I *know*," she said. "I understand now why you refused to study magic. You were clearing the way for Cassandra, weren't you?"

He swallowed visibly. "You've always been quick at putting things together."

"And I admire your decision. Truly." It took all of her control to keep her head high and her gaze locked with his in the glass. "But I cannot allow you to judge *my* decision now."

"Of course you have to marry a mage," Jonathan said. "I've always known that. But Llewellyn—"

"I *don't care* how good he is at magic!" Amy

snapped. "You don't need to be *the best* to do well in any field, and you know that as well as I do. Just look at half the husbands of the Boudiccate! Your father may have been a brilliant mage, but not all of them are. They don't have to be."

"But they should," Jonathan said, his jaw locked. "Cassandra *is*."

"Then it's a pity I don't wish to marry *her*—argh!" Amy let out a groan even as the inane words escaped her mouth.

Good God. What was he doing to her? She *never* lost her temper so foolishly! She squeezed her eyes shut for one anguished moment.

When she opened them again, Jonathan's lips were twitching. "I'll let her know of that terrible disappointment," he said gravely. "Never fear: she's currently madly in love only with magic, so you needn't worry about breaking *her* heart, too."

"I should think not." Amy gave a rueful shake of her head. She couldn't look away from his reflected blue eyes, now so full of warmth and humor. It felt too good to feel his gaze holding hers—to feel that indefinable, inexorable connection beneath the skin.

Once she wed, and moved out of Harwood House, it would become easier. It had to. When she no longer saw him every day...

No. Her heart clenched. She couldn't think about that now—not if she wished to hold to her purpose. "You know how the world works," she said softly.

"I do." His lips twisted. "That...is why I'd never even

imagined you would consider me as an option in the first place."

The moment felt as fragile as glass held between them.

Cassandra's voice shattered it. "*There* you both are!" She burst breathlessly between them. "Have you told her yet? What did she say?"

Jonathan gave a start and then winced. "Ah, yes." He gave Amy an apologetic look. "The reason I came to find you in the first place."

"You haven't even *mentioned* it?" Cassandra demanded. "What on earth have you two been discussing this whole time?"

For one paralyzed moment, Amy's mind went blank.

Then she said brightly, "The upcoming demonstrations—"

...Just as Jonathan said, "Refreshments!"

"Oh." Cassandra heaved a weary sigh. "*I* see. You two were flirting again." She cast her eyes up to the arched ceiling. "Well, if I'm the only one who's even going to *try* to save this evening...!"

"Save it?" Amy stiffened. "From what?" Her mind was already whirling through possibilities. Had one of the guests said something unmentionable to the Fae ambassadress? Had one of the mages done something disastrous to the drinks?

If Mrs. Seabury had 'accidentally' smacked the Head of the Great Library with her walking stick *again*...

"Father's spell," said Cassandra. "It's on the verge of cracking if we don't fix it *now*."

"What?" Amy's heartbeat lurched. As her head spun, she yanked her gaze back to Jonathan. "And you didn't even bother to *mention*—?"

"She didn't tell me what she needed you for!" His already-fair skin had paled at the news. "She only said that she wanted to talk to you privately."

"Because I didn't want to waste time repeating myself!" Cassandra said impatiently. "First, we have to get everyone out of here, and then—"

"Wait." Amy held out one hand, forcing herself to take steady breaths even as the walls tightened around her. All those gallons—tons?—of lake water pushing in against them, only waiting to swallow them all the very moment the spell shattered... "None of the other mages here have noticed any particular danger tonight." Even Mr. Westgate hadn't considered the matter imminent, had he?

"Because *they* don't know Father's spell, of course." Cassandra rolled her eyes. "Do you think Mother would ever let any of *them* near his private papers?"

"But she let *you*?" Amy pointedly raised her eyebrows.

The younger girl's skin flushed, but her jaw firmed stubbornly even as she dropped her gaze. "I found my own way in," she muttered. "Just ask Jonathan if you don't believe me."

Jonathan's silent nod was confirmation enough.

"Very well." Amy took a deep breath, adjusting to

the news. Was she only imagining the creak of the rounded windowpane nearby, as if it were suddenly facing excess pressure?

Surely that was pure imagination. And yet...

"We'll have to be as discreet as possible," she said, even as she cringed internally at the thought of it.

Where were all two hundred of the guests going to *go*? The ballroom inside Harwood House hadn't been used for any public functions in decades. Not only had it not been decorated for tonight, but it had fallen into the most casual of family usage across the years. As Amy imagined the reactions of every visiting dignitary to being shuffled inside tonight to find its thirty-year-old decorations and tattered, comfortable chairs piled with newspapers around the fireplace...

What excuse *could* possibly explain that, apart from the truth?

But Miranda... "What did your mother say when you told her?"

Only silence answered Amy's question.

"I beg your pardon?" Amy's eyes widened. "You haven't even *tried* to tell her?"

"She wouldn't listen to me!" Cassandra's face flushed deeper. "I couldn't even get her away from the group that she was talking to. And if I'd dared utter the word 'spell' to her in front of all of them..." She shook her head, her fists clenching at her sides. "You're the only one who might actually get her to pay attention."

"I...see." And Amy did see, all too well.

Oof. Well, she had promised Miranda to deal with

any dramas that arose tonight, even if this wasn't quite the sort of excitement that either of them had had in mind.

How long did they have before the spell gave way?

Amy squared her shoulders. "Right," she said briskly. "Cassandra, you need to find Mr. Westgate and tell him *exactly* what you've just told me. Beg him, on your mother's behalf, not to share your secret with anyone else, but when you are speaking privately with him, don't hold a single detail back."

"Will he believe me?"

"Probably not," Amy admitted. "But he's the only one I know who's already worried about the spell, so he's the most promising mage for you to approach. In the meantime, I'll find your mother—and Jonathan, would you please start charming all of the non-mages outside for an evening walk around the grounds? You can tell them we've decided to hold tonight's magical demonstrations on the lakeshore tonight, to take advantage of the weather."

"Of course." He moved away without another word, heading for the closest group of fan-wielding politicians.

Cassandra hung back one more moment, her face taut with anxiety. "Do you...are you certain you can't come with me to talk to Westgate? If—"

"Don't worry," Amy said firmly. "I'll tell your mother that you did it only under my instructions."

Miranda might well not forgive her for that—and the plausibility of that result was enough to make

Amy's stomach twist with a sickening mixture of loss and shame.

But Amy had been given charge of all of the details for tonight, and that meant protecting everyone in this ballroom, no matter how she had to do it. So as Cassandra darted off, Amy lifted her chin and set off to tell her mentor everything that Miranda Harwood would least like to hear from her tonight.

She was halfway across the room when Llewellyn caught up with her. This time, he didn't physically take hold of her; clearly, he was capable of learning that sort of lesson, which she filed away as a promising sign for their joint future. But his voice rippled with impatience as he said, "Finally! I thought he'd never be finished with you. What was he nattering on at you about before his sister arrived? If—"

"My lord." Amy didn't slow her stride across the room, her fey-silk skirts swishing purposefully around her long legs. "I am glad to see you. I need your help quite urgently."

"You...do?" She heard the frown in his voice, although she didn't take the time to look around. "With what?"

"Can you cast a spell to amplify my voice? I'd like to make an announcement." She could already sense a ripple in the crowd as Jonathan worked his own, good-humored form of magic on the various guests, but he couldn't possibly make his way through the entire crowd in time.

"I thought you wanted to wait until after the demonstrations?"

"What?" She took one baffled second to absorb his words—then realized what he meant. "Oh, no, *that* isn't the announcement that I meant. No, this is urgent. Can you help me with it quickly, please?"

He let out an irritated huff of air. "Perhaps if you would slow down and take the time to give me the courtesy of a proper explanation, so that I could make my own decision about the matter—"

"Never mind." It was only a few more steps—

There. She came to a halt, smiling serenely, in front of Lord Cosgrave, Lady Cosgrave's good-natured husband, who was standing gossiping with a group of fellow mages. "My dear Lord Cosgrave. Would you do me the favor of providing me with a moment of amplification?"

He slanted a startled look at Llewellyn, but stepped forward agreeably. "Of course, Miss Standish." Murmuring something under his breath, he gestured toward her—and Amy felt a sudden, thrumming power in her chest. *Perfect.*

"My lords and ladies and distinguished visitors," she said brightly, and all of the music and chatter broke off as her voice rang around the circular ballroom. "May I have your attention? On behalf of Mrs. Harwood, I'd like to invite every lady and non-mage among our guests to enjoy a delightful evening stroll around the Aelfen Mere. The musicians will accompany all of you to perform in the open air for your enjoyment whilst the mages remain here to prepare for their demonstrations afterward. If you could all move as quickly as possible, please, our marvelous mages would deeply appreciate your assistance. Thank you!"

She finished with a confident nod and a discreet silencing gesture in Lord Cosgrave's direction. His own nod, a moment later, confirmed that the spell had been safely removed. "Thank you," she told him in her own normal tones, and spun on her heel as a genteel queue formed for the marked exit point on the tiled floor.

This time, she didn't have nearly as far to go. Miranda Harwood was already aiming for her through the shifting crowds, a pleasant, social smile pinned to her lips.

"What in the world is going on?" Miranda murmured under her breath as they met, squeezing closely together to make space for the stream of chattering guests. "An evening stroll by the lake for all of them, together? We haven't even set fey lights about the perimeter, much less—"

"I needed an excuse," Amy murmured back even more softly. "It's a matter of magical safety, and we need the mages to fix it before we can allow anyone back inside the ballroom."

"Oh?" Miranda looked past Amy to Llewellyn, who'd followed her. "Lord Llewellyn, can you explain the particular magic that's involved?"

"Don't ask me, Mrs. Harwood." His smile was decidedly strained. "Miss Standish hasn't chosen to share those details with me, either. Apparently, my expertise was not desired."

Ouch. Amy stifled a wince. "There wasn't time for explanations, I'm afraid. I've been notified of an urgent magical crisis, and—"

"From whom?" Llewellyn frowned. "The only people you've talked to since our dance were Harwood and his sister, and neither of them..."

Amy could see the exact moment when Miranda realized the answer to that question. It was the first time she'd ever seen her mentor pale.

The sudden look of horrified vulnerability on Miranda's face felt unbearable—and the fact that she had caused it, even more so. But Amy kept her gaze fixed steadily upon her mentor as she said quietly, "It doesn't matter exactly how I found it out. The point is, the spell that keeps this ballroom safe is on the verge of shattering for good. If we don't find a way to fix it quickly—"

"Is this whole fuss about old Westgate's cawing?" Llewellyn gave a dismissive snort of laughter. "Mrs. Harwood, as I told Miss Standish earlier—"

"It was explained to me—persuasively—by someone whose magical opinion I trust." Amy kept her voice low and gentle and very clear as she watched the different emotions flash across Miranda's face. "The only step we can take at this point is to evacuate the non-mages as swiftly as possible. Mr. Westgate has already been informed, and I'm sure he'll direct the other officers of magic who are in attendance tonight."

"Without the original spell to hand?" Llewellyn shook his head impatiently. "No, no. Even if you *were* right, that would be impossible. You may be an expert in standing around talking people into trade agreements and suchlike, Miss Standish"—his upper lip curled in undisguised disdain—"but when it comes to the *manly* issues in life, you may trust my assurance that no one in this ballroom could possibly bolster the original spell without knowing *exactly* what it said in the first place. So unless you happen to be keeping it here...?"

Miranda moistened her lips, her voice hoarse. "My husband's spellwork is all safely locked within his study, which cannot be entered by magic. Neither can the corridor around it. It would take twenty minutes, at the very least, to retrieve it—and of course, they'd also have to look through all of his collected spells to find the right one. If—"

Creeeeeeaaaaak!

Every muscle in Amy's body twinged with unmistakable recognition. She certainly hadn't imagined *that* sound coming from the rounded walls. As she looked at the social stream of guests making their unhurried ways to the exit point before they left, vanishing only two at a time with well over a hundred still left in the queue, a sick sense of certainty coiled into place within her.

"We don't have that much time." *I'm sorry*, she added silently to the woman who'd meant more to her than any other authority figure in her life. *I would never*

53

betray you intentionally. "There is," she said, "one person who knows that spell intimately. So she'll have to be your reference for tonight's work."

Miranda's eyes shut. She didn't faint; she didn't even stagger. She was one of the strongest women in all Angland, and even the ruin of her only daughter's reputation and the legacy that she had worked all her life to pass forward couldn't overwhelm her now.

But when she opened her eyes again, there was a lost look in them that Amy had never seen before, even as her lips stretched into an unconvincing smile. "Well," she said briskly, "we'd best get to work, then. Shall we?"

Mr. Westgate was already making his way through the crowds towards them, surrounded by three other mages Amy recognized...and by Cassandra, who held herself with rigid control as she followed them, as if she were suppressing herself with difficulty. "Mrs. Harwood." Westgate's nod was perfunctory, but it didn't appear to be an insult; he had the look of a man deeply involved in a challenging puzzle. "If you would kindly vacate the ballroom for your own safety—"

"I beg your pardon?" Miranda gave a laugh so harsh, it made the closest guest glance around with wide eyes. "Mr. Westgate, you're here because my husband's wedding gift to me is failing, and..." Her smile twisted as she looked around the growing group of mages that now surrounded them, drawn from all across the room. "My daughter," she said with bitter clarity, "has just exposed a truth that was *never* meant to be known outside our family. Do you really expect me to leave now as if none of this were my business?"

Westgate's eyebrows rose at her words; then he shrugged. "We'll speak frankly, then. In order to fix this spell, we'd have to trust that both your daughter's recollection *and* her interpretations of it are correct—and as both of those points are exceedingly unlikely..."

Cassandra's face reddened—but it was Amy who stepped forward until she stood toe-to-toe with the Boudiccate's foremost officer of magic. "Mr. Westgate," she said coolly, "you may trust *me* when I tell you that I have the utmost faith in Miss Harwood's capability, and so should you. Would you doubt the strength or perspicacity of any other Harwood mage?"

Next to her, Lord Llewellyn's mouth was opening and closing distractingly, like a landed fish struggling to breathe. "She—what—*mage*—? *What*?!"

Westgate's eyes narrowed. "Miss Standish," he began, in the resolute tone of a man about to take control of a rather nasty situation.

Amy sailed across his words with ease. "Her magical lineage is every bit as impressive as her political lineage, as you know perfectly well. It may be a trifle out of the ordinary that her family's magical inheritance has chosen to express itself through a lady for the first time in this generation, rather than choosing her brother..."

"A *trifle*?!" Llewellyn's tone was strangled.

"But as you are all aware," Amy continued firmly, "we have no time for fussing over propriety at this moment. I understand that gentlemen are the more emotional sex, but I have utter faith that you will all rise above the frailties of your natures to show the world exactly how impressive your magecraft is tonight."

Creeeeeakkkkk!

"...Preferably," Amy finished, "before the roof falls in on all of us. If we could possibly save the gentlemanly swoons for afterwards?"

"Gladly." Westgate's tone was grim, but Amy didn't miss the grudging amusement in his eyes. *There.* She'd known she liked him, after all.

Sighing heavily, he turned to face the other mages, whose faces were a picture of mingled outrage and confusion. "Gentlemen, we'll have to split our forces in two. Cosgrave, why don't you lead a force of six in removing the rest of the guests safely from this ballroom? We can't afford to wait for them to leave on their own. As for the rest of us..." His jaw set, but he showed the inner strength that she'd glimpsed earlier as he visibly forced himself to turn to Cassandra. "Why don't you guide us through that spell, Miss Harwood?"

Perfect. Amy stepped back, gracefully making way for the mages to all gather around the younger girl's small figure.

Anyone else of her age, in such a situation, might have quailed or frozen at their hostile looks; but Cassandra was a Harwood through and through, and she'd been raised by a mother who faced down powerful opponents every day. Pride rose in Amy's chest as she watched Cassandra meet each questioner's skeptical gaze and heard the clarity of the girl's recitation.

It was all gibberish to Amy's ears, of course, but the confidence and authority of Cassandra's tone shone through the unfamiliar terminology; and when an older mage broke in with a sneering remark, Cassandra's quick retort made two of the younger mages laugh appreciatively.

Amy didn't need to look around to sense the intensity of Miranda's gaze upon her daughter. "She is remarkable," Amy said softly. "Schooling that entire group of grown mages without a qualm..."

"She could have ruled the Boudiccate." Miranda's voice was thick with emotion. "She *should* have ruled the Boudiccate. But after tonight..."

"Oh, Miranda." Amy couldn't help turning around at the anguish in her mentor's voice. *Perhaps...*

No. This was one crisis that she couldn't fix. No matter how hard she tried, even Miranda herself could never convince the full mass of assembled mages in this ballroom to forget the insult of her daughter's trespass into their territory. There was absolutely no chance of Cassandra Harwood ever entering politics after tonight.

But then again...

Amy stilled as a new idea flowered within her—an idea that would never have occurred to her before she'd met the Harwood family and begun to glimpse shocking and world-changing possibilities outside the security of tradition.

Earlier this evening, when the concept had first occurred to her, she'd named it impossible to herself. After all, *no one* had ever done it before in all of Anglish history. And yet, as she looked now across the tiled floor at the mosaic of Boudicca herself, past the group of mages listening with grudging respect to Cassandra's words, she could almost imagine that ferocious mother to their nation giving her a knowing wink.

Had Boudicca ever let tradition stop *her*?

How the Romans must have laughed, all those centuries ago, at the very idea of a woman—a mere widow to an insignificant king—rising up to overthrow their imperial rule and send them fleeing from the island in humiliation. That, too, must have been inconceivable to them. But once Boudicca had found a partner to her political and martial prowess in the magic of her second husband...

They had set a mold for the ages with their epic partnership. But they had broken earlier rules to do it —and they broke even more when they started their radical new nation in the wake of the Romans' expulsion.

Amy had always yearned for a family and a place of her own; she'd always believed that following the accepted rules was the only reliable way she could ever possibly achieve it.

But she'd always sworn that once she did find a

family of her own, she would do anything it took to protect them. What if—despite every expectation— she had already found that family after all? If those stuffy old unquestioned rules were all that was stopping her from taking her rightful place within it...

Well. What could any politician want more than to change her nation for the better? She'd already known that this would be the most important evening of her life to date. She only hadn't known why, until this moment.

"Miranda," Amy said firmly to her mentor, "you're wrong about Cassandra. She would have been a terrible politician."

Shock flashed across the older woman's face. "I beg your pardon?"

"When has she ever enjoyed compromise or negotiation?" Amy demanded. "And just listen to her now." She tilted her head toward the stream of information spinning from the girl's mouth. "When has she *ever* absorbed that level of detail—or even made the slightest attempt!—in any of the subjects you've forced down her across the years?"

Miranda's jaw tightened. "She's still young," she grated. "She could have outgrown—"

"Did your husband ever outgrow those interests?" Amy asked gently.

She had seen the portrait of Mr. Harwood in Miranda's study—and she had seen an identical look of confident genius in his daughter's face, too, tonight.

Miranda clearly had as well. Her gaze dropped.

When she spoke again, her voice was low and bitter. "What could be the purpose in trying to judge such matters? The world will crush her if she tries to stand against it."

"Not if we don't let it." For the first time ever, Amy let her tone ring with authority over her mentor.

Her admiration for Miranda Harwood would never change. Nor would her love and gratitude; but after a lifetime of supervising the world as it was, how could it *not* be nigh-on impossible for Miranda to imagine that world turning upside down? To conceive of such an outright transformation, one required a younger generation with fresh eyes—and Miranda's own children had supplied that in spades.

Together, the Harwood siblings had shown Amy how to imagine new possibilities outside the norm. But neither of them would ever move in the political realm —which meant that she, alone, might be the only person who could make those possibilities take shape for them both...and win an undreamed-of victory for herself along the way.

"What if," she said, holding her mentor's gaze, "we make *this* tonight's magical demonstration after all?"

Miranda frowned. "You mean, we summon all of the guests back to the ballroom to witness it?"

"No," Amy said, "but we'll tell them *exactly* what happened here afterwards—in great detail. And then we'll send the announcement to the newspapers ourselves."

Miranda's eyes narrowed. "Rather than attempting

to hide the news, which would be a lost cause regardless..."

"We shall brag about it *shamelessly*," Amy finished with deep satisfaction. "Because *of course* it would be a Harwood woman who finally broke the bounds of tradition to excel in magic above every adult mage assembled here! As they all admitted themselves—and we'll make very certain to repeat that in our statement —not even all of them together could have fixed the spell here, tonight, without her expertise."

A smile began to tug at Miranda's lips. "Oh, *yes*." Her eyes began to dance as the pleasure of the game finally overcame her shock and grief and fear for her daughter's future. Amy had *known* her mentor would see the way once a real opening was placed before her! "We'll be sure to quote Mr. Westgate himself on the matter," said Miranda. "Won't *that* be a lovely paragraph to read in all of the morning papers? And as Cassandra will have publicly proven herself to be one of the most astonishing new talents in magery..."

"Let the Great Library try to keep her out now!" Amy's grin was as fierce as the one painted on the great Boudicca herself. *That* great leader had faced down an army of Roman soldiers and the Roman empire itself; with their combined powers of persuasion *and* the newspapers on their side, Amy and Miranda could certainly take on a mere college of mages.

Miranda gave a sudden wince. "Of course, the Boudiccate won't like it, either. Once magic is opened up to women, after all..."

"*Not* to women," Amy said firmly. "To just one extraordinary girl—the single, shining exception in our history who saved the assembled Boudiccate from certain death tonight. They can call her the exception that proves the rule...*unless* they choose to stand against her and turn the matter into fodder for an open debate through all the newspapers."

Miranda let out a low laugh of delight. "Of course!" she said. "Can you imagine the letter columns? That's exactly how I'll put it to them. If they don't want it to turn into a wildfire that rages until *far* wider-reaching reforms are called for..."

"What in the world—?!" Lord Llewellyn's sputtering voice broke through their warm circle of happy scheming. "Miss Standish!" Glaring at her, he shook his blond head. "You cannot be serious in your intent. If you imagine I could *ever* ally myself with a plan so offensive to any gentleman of dignity and standing—"

"What a pity," Amy said calmly, and gave him a nod of gracious dismissal. "Just as well we hadn't made any announcements after all, then, don't you think? We can part friends and say no more of the matter."

"But—!" He stared at her, blinking. "You can't change your mind now. Once you've given your word as a politician—"

"I," said Amy gently, "haven't given my word on anything—or even made any proposals to be revoked, Lord Llewellyn. Had you forgotten that salient detail?"

His pale cheeks flushed. His jaw worked. "*Everyone* will hear about this disgrace," he snarled. "How you threw away a match that could have brought you everything you'd ever dreamed of..."

"Oh, dear. My *very* dear Lord Llewellyn." Miranda Harwood's tone had quelled generations of stronger mages. "Tsk, tsk." She shook her head gently as she considered him. "To be so afraid of one young lady entering your field? What exactly is it that strikes such fear in your heart, I wonder?"

"Good question, Llewellyn." Jonathan Harwood slipped into place on his mother's other side, his narrowed eyes focused on the other man. The tangible comfort of his presence slipped around Amy like a warm coat, relaxing muscles in her back that she hadn't even realized she'd been clenching. "You don't think my sister might be proven *better* at magic than you, do you, old boy? Because that's certainly what it sounds like to me."

"Harwood!" Llewellyn glowered at him. "Of all the insulting, outrageous—!" Turning his glare around their united semicircle, he snapped, "Miss Standish, I have been grievously mistaken in your character. Everyone will soon understand that I would never even *dream* of accepting any proposals from you now *or* in the future!"

"Of course not," Amy said soothingly. "So I won't embarrass either of us by asking. But don't you think you should go and assist the others? You wouldn't want the papers thinking you had fled in fear, after all."

"*Insupportable!*" Llewellyn gritted through his teeth,

and strode away, visibly seething, to take his place among the other gathered mages.

"Phew!" Miranda gave herself a shake, as if she were ridding herself of a bad smell. "I do beg your pardon, my dear. Clearly, he was *not* the right man for you after all. Have no fear, though. Once we put our heads together, we'll soon find a far better partner for you, and then—"

"Actually..." Amy drew a deep breath and looked past her mentor, her heartbeat suddenly racing in anticipation. *Time to change the world...again.* Her voice came out sounding uncharacteristically breathless. "I believe I've already found him."

Jonathan had looked away, expression tight, at his mother's last words; now he jerked around to meet Amy's gaze, his blue eyes blazing with an intensity that made her breath catch in the most delicious manner.

"What, you've chosen someone else already?" Miranda's eyebrows rose, and she discreetly angled herself to study the group of mages before them. "How beautifully organized of you, as usual. May I ask which of these gentlemen—?"

CREEE-AAAAAAAKKKKKK!

Every voice in the room broke off. Amy's gaze flew to the rounded ceiling. *Oh, no.*

They'd all waited too long after all. Under her horrified gaze, the high panes of glass bent, buckled, and—

"Now, gentlemen!" snapped Mr. Westgate.

Glass shattered. With a roar that resonated through

Amy's bones, water that had been held back for nearly thirty years swept down in a nightmarish torrent. Amy barely even felt herself move as she threw her arms out —for Miranda, for Jonathan, for both of them at once. She felt their arms close around her, too...

And then the water simply stopped twenty feet above their heads. It hung there in perfect silence, catastrophe incarnate waiting to rush down and overwhelm them all.

Amy's harsh, broken breath filled her ears. Still clinging to Miranda and Jonathan, she turned her head...and found Mr. Westgate gesturing a white-faced Cassandra forward while the gentleman mages remained in a semicircle behind her, their arms raised, their jaws clenched with visible effort, and their intent gazes fixed on the water that hung unmoving above them.

Cassandra's face was pale and set. She glanced at her mother, and a flash of pain broke her mask of composure; at her brother, and Amy saw her mouth soften with sudden, heart-stopping anxiety. Then Cassandra looked, with unmistakable desperation, to her.

Finally. This, Amy did know how to handle.

Fixing a calm, confident smile on her own face, Amy ignored the mounting panic within her chest, gave Cassandra the brisk nod that the other girl clearly needed, and then raised her eyebrows in a firm message: *Well? Get on with it!*

There. The younger girl's face eased, and her shoulders settled with visible relief as the uncertainty fell away from her. Nodding back to Amy, Cassandra lifted her arms with all the unshakeable authority of her mother stepping forward to address the assembled Boudiccate of Angland.

Amy held her calm smile with every ounce of strength left in her. *This is really happening.*

Miranda's hand tightened convulsively around her arm. Only Jonathan's hand, warm and steady on Amy's lower back, held her upright in the whirling terror of the moment, like a promise of his own unshakeable certainty.

That was what he did, wasn't it? He kept every woman in his family steady with a deep well of strength that had absolutely nothing to do with either magic or status—and no other touch in Amy's life had ever felt even half so right.

Amy had always known she would do anything to protect her family whenever and wherever she found them. But she'd never imagined just how much they would do for her.

Now Cassandra opened her mouth, her gaze still fixed on Amy's face as if it were a touchstone, and spoke a stream of bright syllables that filled the air with sparking, dancing impossibility. Under Amy's wide, eager gaze, a cloud of stars formed around Cassandra, brighter than any fey-light she'd ever seen.

Goosebumps skated across Amy's skin as those stars massed together and flew to the center of the ballroom...directly above Boudicca's ferocious grin of victory. It was an unmistakable sign, and from Miranda's sudden indrawn breath beside her—and the grim tightening of Mr. Westgate's mouth, when she glanced in his direction—Amy wasn't the only one to have witnessed it.

Another kind of nation-shaking history was being made before their eyes tonight.

Cassandra called out one final word—and as Amy sucked in a breath of awe, the gathered stars *exploded*. Points of light shot outward toward the broken glass and crumbling walls of the underwater ballroom.

Grunts and gasps broke out from the gathered mages as the water flung itself outward, too, apparently wrenching itself from their combined grips. Several of them stumbled in the aftershock, and a few fell to their knees—but Amy had scant attention to spare for any of them as she watched the rounded ceiling reform itself before her eyes, higher and smoother than ever before. Glass panels built themselves out of magic stars.

When she turned, she found stars on Miranda Harwood's cheeks, too—the first tears she'd ever seen from her mentor.

"Isn't it amazing?" Amy breathed. "*She* is amazing."

"She's lost," Miranda whispered. "I'll never get her back. Not now. She..." Breaking off, she gritted her jaw tight.

But she never looked away as the ballroom was rebuilt, even as the tears streamed silently down her face. Amy silently closed her fingers around Miranda's, holding on with all of her love as the world shifted around them.

"See, it's even better than it was before." Jonathan's warm breath rustled against Amy's hair as he spoke. "Just look what she's added over there, Mother."

Miranda blinked, peered—and let out a choked laugh. "That little minx! If your father could only see this..."

Amy couldn't help the gurgle of laughter that escaped her own lips as she followed Jonathan's gesture toward the line of familiar portraits from Anglish history. Now, a portrait of the late Mr. Harwood—a perfect copy of the one that hung in Miranda's study—rose above all the rest, beaming confidently down at the company in the ballroom he'd created. Cassandra herself was painted just beneath him: his magical heir, in every way.

How long had the girl worked before tonight to develop such detailed amendments to this spell? Amy couldn't even hazard a guess. But one conclusion was inescapable.

"You see, Miranda?" she said, squeezing her mentor's hand. "She *has* learned something from you after all. She knows exactly how to make a political statement!"

"Pahh." With a sniff, Miranda dashed the final tears from her face. Taking a deep breath, she lifted her chin.

All around them, the most powerful mages of the realm were racing around the rebuilt ballroom like rowdy, untrained children, calling back and forth to each other in shock, admiration, or dismay as they made note of every detail. Cassandra stood in apparent ease at the center of the chaos, her shoulders and expression perfectly relaxed, but Amy knew her well enough by now to recognize the rebellious glint in her eyes. She was more than ready to take them all on in verbal battle—and if the mages were given enough time to overcome their initial shock, that battle would be both forthcoming *and* disastrous.

"Time for a distraction," she murmured. "Quickly, too."

With a brisk nod, Miranda stepped forward, clapping her hands for silence. "Gentlemen! Would you all be so good as to assist me in bringing back the rest of our guests? I believe we're now ready for your own magical demonstrations of the evening, as my daughter's performance has come to such a satisfactory conclusion."

Aha. Amy grinned inwardly as she watched the gathered and outraged attention of the room swing directly to her mentor, who was more than capable of dealing with it.

Cassandra might not realize it, but she always had her mother on her side—and like Amy, Miranda Harwood would do whatever it took to protect her family.

There was no need to interfere in Miranda's entertainment now. So Amy stayed discreetly in place near the rounded wall, enjoying the impressive spectacle of her mentor putting the gathered ballroom in its place and setting every mage in the room, like it or not, into order. As all the fear, exhilaration and relief of the evening finally streamed out of Amy's body, just one tingling point of physical awareness remained.

Jonathan Harwood hadn't moved, either—and his hand still rested against her lower back.

Standing as they did, facing the rest of the party, no one else could see that single point of contact. His strong fingers hadn't curled against the silk of her dress; she knew they would fall away the very moment she stepped forward.

With every breath, she felt the warmth from his hand spread a little further along her skin, like a sparkling, illicit secret between them. He seemed to be watching the political show with all of his attention; but it only took the slightest sidelong glance to see that his broad chest was rising and falling with his quick, shallow breaths. Amy didn't even bother to bite back her smile of satisfaction at that sight.

Everyone who'd ever read the newspapers knew that Jonathan Harwood was a problem. But after ten months of being twisted round and round by that problem, she finally knew how to solve it.

Amy loved it when she could see exactly the right path for her future stretching before her, only waiting for her to make it all happen.

"Shall we make the announcement tonight?" she asked. "I think it's probably the best timing for everyone, all things considered. That way, we can let all of the shocks collide at once."

"Announce—you mean, Cassandra?" He blinked, his hand falling away from her back. "I rather thought she'd already announced herself."

"Well, of course, *that's* all taken care of," Amy said briskly. "Your mother and I have a plan to deal with that."

"Of course you do." His lips curved appreciatively. "You always do."

"And I like to keep to my plans, too," Amy told him. "You know exactly which announcement I was planning to make tonight."

"*What?*" He shook his head, his eyes widening with horror. "But—but you said..."

"Oh, really, Jonathan." Amy tucked her hand into his arm with an affectionate pat. "Your editors wouldn't believe it if they heard you stammering like this. I'm meant to be announcing my betrothal tonight, don't you recall?"

"Oh, I recall *that* point perfectly well." Jonathan's tone was grim. "But since you've sent Llewellyn packing at last..."

"I'll just have to announce the man I'd really like to wed, instead." She gave him a darting, mischievous grin. "Don't you think that's the only sensible conclusion?"

He stared at her for one speechless moment, his fair skin flushing. Then he shook himself hard and took a step backward, pulling his strong arm free from her grip.

"*No.*" His voice sounded as raw as if it had been scraped over stone. "You can't do this, Amy. I won't let you!"

"Oh, really?" She raised her eyebrows, stalking toward him with predatory delight. "And how do you plan to stop me, exactly?"

"*Amy!*" He raked an impatient hand through his thick hair, creating irrepressible brown tufts that stood upright with outrage as he backed toward the wall. "You were born to be a politician. Just look at what you've accomplished tonight! You can't throw that all aside. Not for me."

"And I won't," she told him with satisfaction.

Only a cruel woman could have enjoyed the unmistakable flash of dismay that passed through his blue eyes at those last words. Did he really think that she'd change her mind about him now? Amy had learned as a child to be intensely conscious of what any observer might think of her—but now, regardless of everyone else in the room, she reached up for a quick, reassuring touch against his faintly stubbled cheek.

"I'm not throwing away *anything*," she told him patiently. "I've only decided to keep you at my side for all of it."

He swallowed convulsively, leaning into her touch. "You can't marry someone else and expect me—"

"*Jonathan!*" At that, she gave up and rolled her eyes,

letting her hand fall to her side. "Are you truly that blinded by the rules? After showing me yourself how to break them?"

He shook his head slowly, his stunned gaze fixed on hers. "*Every* member of the Boudiccate has to be married to a mage. Everyone knows that's the rule."

"Yes, and everyone knew that only men could be mages," she said, "*until tonight*. The rules are changing now, aren't they?" The smile that spread across her face seemed to rise from her very soul, fully liberated at last and ready to spread its wings. "You're the one who started it, all those years ago. You rebel!"

"I'm not the one turning the world inside out tonight." The step he took toward her was only an inch, but she felt it like the promise of victory. "But Amy," he murmured, his breath kissing her forehead, "we can't know that it'll work. Even if we do convince the Great Library to take on Cassandra as a student, the Boudiccate is another matter entirely. You could lose everything because of me!"

"But I won't," she told him firmly. "No matter whether they agree to admit me or not—and you *know* exactly how hard I'll work to persuade them!—I can't possibly lose everything, no matter what they decide. Not if I've gained *you*."

He was the one man in the world whose presence made her feel stronger than she ever had before, ready to take on the world unrestrained by old fears. Who could ever be a better partner for a woman with ambition?

It was time to create her own vision of the future.

"Jonathan Harwood," she said clearly, "will you marry me, share my life, and be my husband forever?"

Her words rang out into a sudden, unexpected silence, just as the mages and Miranda finished their conversation. Every head in the room swung around to stare at them.

Lord Llewellyn's mouth dropped open into a disbelieving "O." Mr. Westgate's eyebrows rose in speculation. Cassandra, still standing alone in the center of the ballroom, broke into a delighted, triumphant grin.

I knew it! she mouthed across the room.

Surrounded by mages, Miranda Harwood blinked in visible shock...then pressed one hand against her lips as her eyes suddenly sparkled with her second tears of the evening. The unhidden joy in her gaze, as she looked across the room at the two of them, was enough to make Amy feel as giddy as if she could rise like a fey-light and float through the air.

"Amy Standish," said Jonathan ruefully before the gathered assembly, "you certainly know how to make a proposal to remember."

"Well, then?" She cocked her head, smiling up at him with delight. "What *is* your answer, for everyone here to witness? Because I *know* you are perfectly capable of saying no to whatever you're asked in front of all the world."

He shook his head slowly, his eyes fixed on hers. "Never to you," he told her. "And I promise you, Amy, I never will."

"Ohhh!" Amy had spent all her life learning poise and self-control. But she wasn't entirely *inhuman*.

After ten months of holding herself back from kissing Jonathan Harwood, she couldn't resist flinging herself into his arms any longer, in full view of their joint family and the most powerful mages of their nation.

Luckily, he welcomed the act with unmistakable enthusiasm...and it turned out that he was *very* good at one particular kind of magic after all.

A NOTE FROM STEPH

Spellswept is a prequel to The Harwood Spellbook, a series of romantic fantasy novellas featuring Cassandra as an adult—and of course Jonathan and Amy, too! The Harwoods *always* stick together.

The series begins with *Snowspelled,* which Ilona Andrews called 'clever, romantic and filled with magic.' I hope you'll enjoy the further adventures of the whole family! The latest novella in the series is *Moontangled*, coming February 3, 2020.

If you can take a few minutes to review *Spellswept* online, I will be really, really grateful. I really love writing this particular series, and honest reviews, whether good or bad (even just one-line reviews!) help *so* much in increasing visibility (and therefore sales). The more people who read these stories, the more of them I can afford to write! :)

If you'd like to stay up-to-date with future stories in this series (and others)—*and* get the chance to win advance copies of future books!—please do sign up to my newsletter:

www.stephanieburgis.com/newsletter

You can get early copies of my ebooks and read my monthly Dragons' Book Club column (where my readers trade fabulous recs of their own!) at my Patreon:

www.patreon.com/stephanieburgis

And you can read excerpts from all of my novels and read many of my published short stories for free through my website: **www.stephanieburgis.com**

CHAPTER ONE

Of course, a sensible woman would never have accepted the invitation in the first place.

To attend a week-long house party filled with bickering gentleman magicians, ruthlessly cutthroat lady politicians, and worst of all, my own infuriating ex-fiancé? Scarcely two months after I had scandalized all of our most intimate friends by jilting him?

Utter madness. And anyone would have seen that immediately...except for my incurably romantic sister-in-law.

Unfortunately, Amy saw the invitation pop into mid-air beside me as we sat *en famille* at the breakfast table that morning. She watched with bright interest as I crumpled it up a moment later in disgust...and then she dashed around the table, with surprising agility despite her interesting condition, to snatch the ball of paper from my hands before I could toss it into the blazing fire where it belonged.

Naturally, I lunged to retrieve it. But I was too late.

The moment she smoothed it out enough to read the details, her eyes lit up with near-fanatical ardor. "Oh, *yes*, Cassandra, we *must* go! Just think: you will finally see Wrexham again!"

"I know," I said through gritted teeth. "That is exactly why we are going to refuse it!"

"Now, love…" Her eyes widened, and she gave me her most innocent look…which put me on guard immediately.

Kind-hearted, loyal, and *adorable* are all phrases that may apply very well to my brother's wife; *innocent* is not one of them, and never has been.

She had, after all, been my mother's final and most promising political protégée.

"I should think," she said now, as if idly, "that you would wish to show everyone how little notice you take of any gossip. After all, if we refuse this invitation, you know everyone will say it was because you were too afraid to see Wrexham again."

My teeth ground together. "I am *not* afraid of seeing Wrexham."

"Well, *I* know that," Amy said, looking as smug as a cat licking up fresh cream. "But does *he*?"

Well. It isn't that I don't know when I'm being managed. But there are some possibilities that cannot be borne. And the thought of my ex-fiancé's dark eyebrows rising in his most fiendishly supercilious look at the news of my cowardly refusal...

I drummed my fingers against the table, searching for a way out.

Behind my brother's outspread newspaper, an apparently disembodied voice spoke. "Better leave early," my brother said. "It's meant to snow next week, according to the weather wizards."

Amy sat back, smiling and resting her hands on her rounded belly...

And that was how the three of us ended up rattling through the elven dales in mid-winter, with the first flakes of snow falling around our carriage.

Find out what happens next in *Snowspelled*, Volume I of The Harwood Spellbook

ACKNOWLEDGMENTS

Thank you so much to Rene Sears, Jenn Reese, Aliette de Bodard, R.J. Anderson, Leah Cypess, Karen Healey, and Patrick Samphire for beta-reading and critiquing this novella. I appreciate it so much!

Thank you to Tiffany Trent, who not only co-edited the anthology where it first appeared but also patiently and thoroughly edited and copy-edited this story. Any mistakes remaining are entirely my own!

Words can't express how grateful I am to Ravven, who designed the gorgeous cover of this ebook for me as a holiday gift. (!!!) Ravven, your work is amazing and I know exactly how lucky I am to have received this gift. Thank you so much!

And as always, thank you so much to every reader who's supported this series. It means a LOT to me!